THE GATHERING

Sarah Singer

THE
GATHERING

WILLIAM L. BAUHAN, PUBLISHER
DUBLIN, NEW HAMPSHIRE

Copyright © 1992 by Sarah Singer
Library of Congress Cataloguing in Publication data:
Singer, Sarah
The gathering / by Sarah Singer.
   p.   cm.
ISBN 0-87233-102-4
I. Title
PS3569.I574G38   1992
811'.54—dc20   91-18264
                                                     CIP

Printed in the United States of America.
This book was typeset in Bembo by EDC, Chicopee, Mass.
and printed and bound by Thomson-Shore, Inc., Dexter, Michigan.
Designed by W.L. Bauhan.

For Leon
More—In Memoriam

Acknowledgments

Grateful acknowledgement is made to the publications in which
some of these poems appeared:

The Lyric for Geraniums in August, Less Than Shadow,
Home Movie, Equestrian Park Statue, Winter Come of Age,
Mrs. Lincoln Speaks of Ann Rutledge, and Now in October;
The Round Table for Guinevere, the Nun; *Jewish Frontier* for The
Gathering; *Voices International* for Pin Oak, Errant Flower, Upon
My Demise, Aubade, Waiting for the Diagnosis, Convalescence,
Mary Shelley Mourns Her Husband, Nineteenth Century Quilt,
and Where Small Birds Preen; *Bitterroot* for Letter from M.,
Moving Day, Portrait of My Aunt, Waking, Scene of Accident,
and Love Song; *The Fiddlehead* and *The Diamond Anthology* of
The Poetry Society of America for The Mad Librarian; *Chicago
Jewish Forum* for Sabbath Portrait; *Judaism* for Ruth.

The Mad Librarian appeared in somewhat abbreviated form in
The Diamond Anthology and in my earlier book, *After the
Beginning*.

Edge of Night appeared in *The New York Times*, copyright
1957 by The New York Times Company. Reprinted by
permission.

Autistic Girl is reprinted with permission from *Yankee
Magazine*, Dublin, New Hampshire.

This Lake, My Garden originally appeared, 1989, on the
Home Forum Page of *The Christian Science Monitor*.

Contents

IV. *Where Small Birds Preen*

I

A Sheaf of Lilies

Sestina for L.

What sleight of hand, what glittering amulet
Can unspell time, and redefine your being
To utmost presence? Here, alone in your garden
Where bees invade the sanctum of the rose,
And favor cyclamen you grew from seed,
I touch what your hands praised, but find no ease.

Even beneath this oak where you found ease,
The hours clock loss, your name no amulet
To conjure or elate. Though puffballs seed
The willing air, and light renews, all being,
Bereft of you, unflowers. Despite the rose,
My senses winter in a leafless garden.

But time was always summer in that garden
Where love itself enjoined an inward ease
Beyond the reach of windflaw. There the rose
Flared ever without sere, both amulet
And quintessential flower that heightened being,
Affinity, our garden, thought, its seed.

Days blossom like a flower you grew from seed,
But I who garner thorns decry this garden
That gleams and resonates with utter being.
What if blue butterflies court petalled ease,
And sweet dews opalesce? No amulet
Can rout despair. I weary of the rose.

And so I fret the wind, and plague the rose,
Reproach the grass, my words like scattered seed
That will not quicken; truth no amulet
To hold or wear. I tend an inner garden
Where only rue may prosper, and unease
That taints all dream night summons into being

With shades of nightmare. Spent, I wake to being
Aware that pristine weather charms the rose
To gossamer, and gentles leaf toward ease;
The fattened seed pod with its gift of seed,
Replete, affirming sequence in this garden
Where I abide, devoid of amulet.

Once love was amulet, was bloom and being,
Each room a garden where the visioned rose,
Not grown from seed, yet proffered silk and ease.

Cassandra

Troy, my city,
Where torches flare
And revelry abounds,
How shall I mourn for you,
Soon not to be?
Though portents roil
The hapless air,
And serpents rise up
From the sea,
Flutes and timbrels
Yet beguile
In banquet halls,
And harpers chant,
And lovers yet make free.

If I am mad,
Then they are madder still
Who wager gold on games,
And feast and brawl,
But do not heed.

Apprised, I thrash
In horrid sleep,
Dream skies are rent,
And waters bleed.

Pin Oak

Yet once more
Before the season turns,
I will commemorate this tree
That profits me with shade
This August noon,
As much for you,
Deprived now of its subsidy,
As for me;
Would indeed persuade
Leaf and bough
To metaphor
As I endure
Between sleep and sleep;
Not to be said aloud
To counter grief or season,
But rather to be stored
Within that private recess
Of my mind
Where I keep
Bits and pieces loss
Has left behind.

A Sheaf of Lilies

At the Vietnam Memorial—Washington, DC

The grasses rock and rock.
The light is dumb,
And does not temper
Marble dark as grief
Or animate dead names;
And I who come
And would pay tribute, bear
A sheaf of lilies
That cannot transcend
The verities of loss.
This ritual of gesture—
To what end—
Save to emblazon
This or that spent name?
Affiliate to none
Inscribed upon this wall,
I mourn, make claim.

Geraniums in August

Before I know, they've run amuck,
Rear upward, gorge on air and light
Just outside my room; so shock

The careful climate I create
For mind and sense with their undue
Disorder and frenetic height,

I almost hear their rampant hue
And cry. On guard, I draw the blind
To shut them out, would disavow

Unease I cannot name behind
My eyes; but manic thoughts invade
My sleep, and rocked where dreams abound,

I am all but slain by nightmare blade
Of leaf, by scarlet renegade.

Less Than Shadow

What eulogy for all your graces shed?
No legend traced on marble can recall
Your subtle colors and your tilt of head,

Or waken those affinities that bred
Your intimate cadences, their rise and fall.
What eulogy for all your graces shed?

No flare of drums, no sound of marching tread
To thunder down the decades, and extol
Your subtle colors and your tilt of head.

Only the chant of litany instead,
And candle flames that blossom, and soon pall.
What eulogy for all your graces shed?

The light and I impoverished and bled.
On whose behalf—acclaimed in ritual
Your subtle colors and your tilt of head

That leafed my untoward days and garlanded?
Now less than shadow on a distant wall,
What eulogy for all your graces shed,
Your subtle colors and your tilt of head?

The Exile

*For Czeslaw Milosz who once said that
as long as he was denied access to his native Poland,
he felt utterly separate and alone.*

Here even the birds are strange. I have no claim,
And set apart, decry the alien air
That never nurtured me or learned my name,
Assail the season, thistle weed and tare
Held close within myself though roses crest
Beneath my window, and flared leaves endow
The birth of light. What matter east or west?
Horizons mock me, roses disavow.
Those dreams are vain that yet illumine sleep.
I reach toward arms that beckon, spell the dark
Like some remembered sacrament; but steep
Of dawn betrays anew, and clock hands mark
The waking hour when wraith and dream succumb,
Grown tenuous as wind, their music dumb.

Errant Flower

To greet the sun,
The azalea wears
A new blossom,
A red balloon
Torn by the wind
From a child's hand,
And tossed here
Upon a branch.

At sudden whim,
I let it stay,
Watch loud birds gleam
And hover, tremble
Lest one alight,
And curled claws pierce
The thin red skin.

Cannot explain why
I manifest concern
Even to myself,
Nor do I question.
Know only this:
I've seen enough
And more of loss,
And need no reply.

This Lake, My Garden

Reflections summer here
Like flowers
In this glittering garden
Seeded by light,
And, tenuous as noon
But opulent, invite
Touch . . . To what avail?
They cannot be held
Or plaited into garlands,
Are soon dispelled
By the merest tide;
Yet, protean
And rarefied,
Are gathered, abound
Beyond time
Within the perfect garden
Of the mind,
And shimmer
Lovelier than lilies.

Yellow Bird, Be Dumb

Here is no time,
And light, attendant between sleep and sleep,
Dispels itself unheeded.
How denote the jangled rhyme
Of madness, the sweep
Of aberration shattering thought and will?
The one of oneness become multiple?
I, Monaghan, divided
In my being, am none
And many, beset
And besetter, my alphabet
Of relevance undone.

Does the house remember,
Or the yellow bird?

Translate them. Fledge
Denuded symmetries of wing and breast
To instancy. Remanifest
The delicate curled claws,
The belled pagoda cage.

Shadow blurs
The doomed light.
Only the yellow bird stirs.
Hush, yellow bird!
And hush, girl with yellow hair!

In the no-time now, I hear what I heard—
The song of the changeling yellow bird;
Girl and bird that mock despair.
Kill the yellow bird, and the girl with yellow hair;
Crush all song in the silken throat
Of the girl with the yellow hair.

Restive bird, your eyes are blind.
Dead songs shudder in the mind,
Of daymare and of nightmare bred.
Be dumb! The sound of sound is dead!

I knew from the beginning
Despite her fleshed pretense and human name,
The plume-stripped breast, the human hands
unpinning
Her yellow-feathered hair, they were the same.
Now bird, now girl, perverse duality,
The dead bird's song upon her lips respun
To frenzied cadences, to stridency
That murdered night, and blotted out the sun;
That sundered self from self, and unclocked time,
That inundated reason, monstrous tune
That stunned all utterance to pantomime—
I killed the girl with hair brighter than noon.

Blind in your dark cocoon
Of death, yellow bird be dumb!

Upon My Demise

Do not weep
Because I cannot know
That wings yet lace the air,
Or how new leaves immerse
Themselves in light.
Instead, on my behalf,
Enjoin recall, and shape
A thought, a flower to verse
No winds may claim
Nor snows impair,
And now and then,
Evoke my name.

Aubade

In this brave interim
After the grace of sleep,
I greet you, tree
That flickers at my window,
Concerned as I
With ebb and flow
Of season, each redefined
And disciplined by light.
How commemorate
This luminous hour
For you, for me,
Our climate yet serene,
Undeterred by ultimates
That bide and hover
Here and just beyond?
To counter time,
Let this verse
Encompass light
And clustered leaf,
Day's bright intent
Of hue and sheen
Become a sacrament.

Letter From M.

M.'s wife was drowned in a boating accident.

I hear it still
Even in sleep,
Neap and swell of water
Tiding over stones.
Again, again
The coot's harsh cry
Above the sound of wind,
The river spelled
And dark, the skies drowned . . .

I stood by
While men in boats
Searched creek and sheltered cove;
Found her weighted down
Among the reeds,
Ferried her ashore
As rain laced the air,
Placed her on the grass.

Unaware
Of grief or love,
She lay at my feet,
Bright limbs in disarray,
Water jeweling throat
And hair like beads.

Moving Day

How shall I say goodbye
To rooms that shaped my days?
These walls do not reply,

Will neither grieve nor praise.
How counter hurt? Would tell
The plangent grass, the rose

We nurtured long and well—
But they heed light and wind
That gentle them or chill.

And this log fence, now vined,
The children straddled, rode
The livelong day, is blind

And mute though each bestowed
Bright presence like a gift.
I speak no word aloud,
Watch shadows lengthen, shift.

II

The Gathering

Portrait of My Aunt

Place her here
Among her flowers,
Grey spill of shawl
Across thin shoulders,
Hands a flicker of white
Among dahlias opulent
With sun, and marigolds,
And bronzed chrysanthemums.
No early hint
Of frost to chasten light,
Perverse October winds
Yet kind. Nothing here
In this Edenic place
That has not quickened
At her touch, finity
Of lustrous frond
And petal, like her own,
Yet held at bay
Though imminence
And utmost veer
Of season will soon shatter
Her delicate pretense.

The Gathering

Summoned in dream
To grandma's house,
They appear,
Sit around the table
On a Sabbath afternoon
Drinking tea.

For each a ritual,
A time for praise,
For ribbon and festoon,
For almonds and sweet cakes
With orange glaze.

Across the decades,
I hear them still,
The women full
Of talk, the uncles tall
And suitably austere,
Who listen, drum
Their fingers on the cloth,
But do not scold
Despite hyperbole
And our uncouth
Childish games.
Graced with Sabbath ease,
They feed and cosset,
Speak our names.

And what of us,
The children who partake
Of bounty and caress,
Envisioned brave

And aureoled,
Our world not yet
In disarray?
I reach out,
Would touch and greet . . .

Evoked in dream
To transcend loss,
Child and elder
Each replete
Beyond the clutch of time
Until I wake.

Abraham and Isaac Climb Mount Moriah

How tall is god? *As tall as light.*
Do mountains grow where God once stood?
Perhaps, my son. For the sacred rite,
I'll bring the fire; you take the wood.

Is God's own voice the voice of wind?
At times, my son. And rain? And grass?
Is all creation hushed or dinned.
You're faint, my father. *It will pass.*

Does God love bird and flower and stone?
Indeed. And does He love the lamb
You bless, then smite? *Will you have done*
At last with babble! We have come

To the sacred place. The sky is rent
With thunder. Why do black wings steep
The air with night? *Child, I am spent . . .*
Father, father, why do you weep?

The Bramble Bush

Behold the bush burned with fire, and the bush was not
consumed. . . . *And the Lord said, "I will send thee unto*
Pharaoh, that thou mayest bring forth my people, the
children of Israel out of Egypt." Exodus III, 2, 7, 10

Cast of Characters

Moses, leader of the Israelites
Zipporah, wife of Moses, daughter of Jethro, priest of Midian
Aaron, brother of Moses
Miriam, sister of Moses and Aaron
The Pharaoh of Egypt

MOSES IN MIDIAN

Enjoined, I leave the others, drive the flock
Across the reach of desert toward the light
That blooms upon Mount Horeb; dune and rock,
Noon-spelled, the air like brass as flames ignite
The bramble bush, and burning, scorch no thorn,
Consume no leaf. Who summons me with claim
I cannot disavow, makes wind a horn?
And there within the bush, who speaks my name?
I hear, am wrung. The ground, made holy, quakes
Beneath my feet as God within that fire
Commands and chides, brooks no refusal, wakes
His thunder to bear witness. Flames expire.
The bramble bush is dumb as birds begin,
And desert creatures fare where God has been.

ZIPPORAH ON THE WAY TO EGYPT

We journey on till dusk, my father's land
And ancient idols forfeit; Moses lost
Within himself despite my outstretched hand,
Cries out in sleep for rite not done, and tossed
In nightmare, grapples, fevered to the bone,
With God and guilt. Lest Moses die, I lift
Our unblest son, take up the sharpened stone
And cut the foreskin, proffer it as gift.
I hush the weeping child, and all but rent,
Await the dawn; at last my husband free
Of taint, redeemed by bloody sacrament,
And fraught with mission. He who cherished me,
Become replete with God; my flesh no more
His dark delight who heard the thorn bush roar.

AARON'S VIGIL

I dreamed of Moses, heard the desert wind
That bruited to itself of miracle
And exodus; dreamed sudden thunder dinned,
And bid me wake as sand dunes blanched like wool,
And light grew tall. Thus summoned, rose, set out
To wait for Moses, certain he would come
To ease our plight as though I heard him shout
My name, apprise of portent like a drum.
A wraith of dust. The sighted caravan,
My brother back from exile; each aware
As we embrace, of privilege, of plan,
And awed by revelation kindled there
Upon the burning bush, I can but heed
And worship, speak for Moses as decreed.

MIRIAM IN GOSHEN

Daylong the sound of weeping, prophecy
And talk of flight derided; Aaron spurned
And Moses vilified as new decree
Afflicts, and miracle of bush that burned
Grows ever more remote. I too maligned
As they petition Pharaoh, dare not praise
My brothers at whose bidding skies go blind
In Egypt, water bleeds, and hailstone slays.
As promised, we are spared. Here field and well
Are undefiled, and morning light renews,
Our own herds hale though Egypt's cattle swell
With plague and die. Yet Pharaoh does not choose
To heed, and we endure till God strikes down
Both servant's child and heir to Egypt's crown.

PHARAOH MOURNS HIS SON

My son is dead, but I must stay my hand,
Dare not destroy this Moses lest his God
Who smites both king and plowman should demand
Yet greater retribution while unshod
And reeking slaves exult, and their sons wake
When mine is stone; ancestral gods implored
To no avail though invocations shake
The temple walls, and sacred draughts are poured.
My councilors entreat, and all concur
That Israel prevails, my crown but dust,
My armies vain. Become petitioner
For mercy, king now beggar for a crust
From slave and recreant, I must agree
To summon Moses, yield to infamy.

We go from Pharaoh, spent but jubilant,
Return to Goshen where the people wait,
And rally those who falter; cull what scant
Provisions are at hand, and mediate
And chastise and enjoin; assemble tribe
And flock as waking birds dispel the stars,
And dews begin; impatient now as scribe
Takes count, and tents are stowed, and water jars.
At last the journey. Some lament, some pray;
The line of march for man and laden beast
Across the dunes; the Lord before us day
And night till all who doubt His being have ceased
Their babble, and give thanks; what dreads within,
Lest I should fail, kept close from God and kin.

Samson

In sleep, I woo her still though nightmare blurs
The flicker of her hands, and murk of dream
Cannot define her mouth. How best recount
Delilah's silken ways that summered heart
And mind? My senses reeled, all counsel shunned
That dared to chasten. Sighted, I grew blind
Before the Philistines gouged out my eyes,
And flung me, shackled, yoked, among the slaves.
Sweet blindness, that, within her faithless arms!
In my delirium, I shut out God,
Disdained all purpose, abrogated prayer
Like some besotted fool. See how they mock
Me now, the cursed rabble and their priests,
And even she whose ardors so regaled,
Who yet confounds my sleep with love and hate,
But I endure. Today they keep me close
Beside the temple walls, assault my ears
With hectic drums and timbrels, Dagon praised
And Yahweh's truth profaned by obscene rites
And bouts of revelry. If I could crush
Those impious throats, and ravage Dagon's house,
Have done with idols and idolaters. . . .
I brace my hands against the pillars, bone
And sinew racked as I petition God
To sanctify this Nazarite once more. . . .
What prescience stirs? What heave of limb affirms
Deliverance and doom? Walls thunder down
Upon their heads and mine. I die, redeemed.

Ruth

Familiar and alien,
They cannot comfort me,
Well-meaning hands
That reach out,
Would reclaim.
For what is Moab
To me now
Who loved Naomi's son
And wed his faith?
Unbeguiled,
I cannot return
To outworn dreams,
To outworn gods whose mouths
Are dumb.

No longer Mahlon's wife,
I risk rebuff,
Yet I will importune
Naomi and her kin
To let me house
In Bethlehem,
And heed their ways.
I seek only to partake
Of gleaner's husk,
Shared gift of bread
Or barley cake.

The Witch of Endor

*King Saul is suddenly afraid because he can no longer
communicate with God. Although he has banished all
wizards, he seeks out the woman who deals with
"familiar spirits," and begs her to call up the seer,
Samuel, from his grave in order to ask his advice. Samuel
denounces Saul, and predicts he and his sons will die in
battle.*

Bereft of pride, he whimpers like a child
Assailed by nightmare; Israel's anointed,
Robed in glory, now suppliant at my feet,
And faint of heart. No longer fraught with God,
The king petitions me in his despair
To summon up the shade of Samuel
From the regions of the dead. How comfort him
As Samuel reviles and thunders doom?
Would take his stricken head upon my breast,
And rock away his grief, were he not king,
And I, imputed witch . . . Can only weep
For Saul and all of Israel, I too
Undone, the taste of ashes in my mouth.

III

The Mad Librarian

Home Movie
For M.L.

Graced beyond time,
You beckon, shimmer
Across the screen,
Your calendar
Forever set at summer;
The honeyed light
Like balm on limb
And lift of throat,
Your mouth serene.

No winds beset.
What shadows brim
The edge of afternoon
Defer to crystal
Attitudes of weather,
And you, among dahlias
And white lilies,
Are tempered, give praise.

To what end?
Tenuous as breath,
Flower and perfect season
Long since forfeit,
And you, for all your wit,
No more than wraith.

Waking

Light clatters,
Raps upon the shutters,
Chastens my fragile bones.

Just outside,
Grasses fret,
Tell their griefs to stones.

Beyond the reach of hands,
You cannot know
I chide the wind
That does not speak your name,
And rue the leaf-clad
Unconcern of season
Light condones.

Even the Birds

This poem is for you,
Grandma, whose voice
Caressed my name,
Who tendered love
And the benediction
Of bread and butter
As soon as I came.

We'd speak of your shtetl,
And how you baked bread
When your children were small,
And hid the extra loaves.
"There was never enough," you said.
"Before the week was out,
They'd found them all."

Assured me: "Child,
That was long ago.
There's enough now."
Would pour milk
Into a tall glass,
And fuss and flutter
Around me yet again.

Today, replete,
My children hoard buns
And leftover bread
To toss out on the snow.
Ours such surfeit,
I wish you could know
Even the birds are fed.

Waiting for the Diagnosis

I cradle my fear,
Lullaby
This untoward child
I cannot dispossess
As waters roil
And crest beyond
My window, and gulls
Ride the light.

I rock and rock
My fear. It wakes
And sleeps at will,
No whit beguiled
By lift of tide
Or windward flight.

Yet again,
I bid it hush
As spinning tides recede.
Unabashed,
This restive child
Does not heed.

Convalescence

All afternoon,
Swans in feathered coats
Drift across the lake
No whit impaired
By winter chill.
Only a few boats
Ride out the wind,
Reeling gulls tossed
In their wake.

I who wear
No coat of white down,
Cower behind walls,
Heart and mind
Concerned with frost.

Though senses drowse,
And limbs demur,
Clad in my thin gown
Of human skin,
I too shall bear
The brunt of squall
And unapt weather,
Must forgo
Balm and billowed ease,
Accede to snow.

Autistic Girl

Nothing here remembers
How it was
In that simple time
When light beckoned
Nearby and beyond
The spelled trees,
And she would come
To stand beside me,
Rapt with wing and flower.
Love summered us,
Braced and quickened
That bright interim
Before she chose
The dark cocoon
Of self, and shut out all
Who sought to importune.
Where her footfalls
Sound no more,
Though I reclaim
And weed and prune,
This sprawl of grass,
No more than I
Or belled forsythia,
Is cognizant of why
She stands alone
Where seasons have no name.

Journal Entry—March 15

Soothsayer to Caesar: Beware the ides of March.
Julius Caesar, Act I, Scene II—William Shakespeare

In the uncertain light,
Trees rear up
To taste the wind.
Shadows steep
And flicker, too soon
Invite the dark.
What votive rite,
What spell or shibboleth
Can counter portent,
And mute those echoes
That assail the stark
Corridors of afternoon
To herald woes?
Caesar in his pride
Once mocked this fateful day,
And bled and died.
Though I am diffident
And would obey,
My meek head bare
Of laurel wreath,
Must I too beware?

The White Stone

She'd found it long ago
Where it had lain
Hidden among roots
And tangled skeins of grass
Behind the house,
Had fingered it like precious ore
From some rich vein
She had not tapped before,
Nor would again.

Blind to the touch and dumb,
It yet endowed
Childhood mind and sense,
Had become
Prize and amulet
That nurtured fantasy;
Would charm her dawns,
Elate her afternoons,
And held or pocketed,
Engender filigreed
Palaces of light
On peaks of amethyst
East of the sun,
West of the moon.

Here and now,
Undone by time,
She takes up the white stone
As though it beckoned still,
Could retrieve
Illusive kingdoms all her own
That shimmered on a distant shore,
But rune and arcane rhyme
Wake no drums,
Spell no more.

Mary Shelley Mourns Her Husband

Percy Bysshe Shelley drowned July 8, 1822.

I dream of hands that cannot claim,
Of days too briefly garlanded
With love and verse; would speak your name,
But thunder lives within my head,

And bred of nightmare, storm birds cry,
And harsh sea sounds offend my sleep
Like some demented lullaby.
Nightlong, griefs crest, and steep and steep

Till I wake, groping toward the light
That does not bless, but quivers down
From shingled eave and windowed height
To inundate . . . I drown, I drown.

Equestrian Park Statue

He rides the air to no applause
Save that of leaves, corrosive bloom
On uniform and rigid jaws.

No one remembers any more
Just why they put him here, what doom
Or glory found him in what war;

And if bemedalled deeds were hailed
Once long ago with pennant, plume,
The Sunday saunterers regaled

By season hardly spare a glance.
While park attendant wields his broom,
Hooves rear in silent dance.

Scene of Accident

After the weeping
And the disbelief,
What do I seek here
In this utmost place
Where all your music died,
And light dreams,
Rarefied,
Unapprised of loss?
To counter griefs
That yet portend,
I speak your name,
Exhort recall
Because I must;
But roadside grass
Concerns itself with wind,
And rapt with dewfall,
Does not listen.

The Mad Librarian

How tall is light that stretches to the sun
Unwalled and free?
Forgotten now in wherefores and in whys.
This room makes finite all infinity,
Squaring the circle of each day undone,
And shutting out the pageant of the skies.
Lost, forever lost to me
The black-winged flight of clouds across the moon.
Locked in the mind,
The darkness merges with the afternoon,
Today with yesterday, before with soon;
Since walls are blind,
I cannot know how broad horizons are,
Or how the light is filtered from a star,
How time is hung in space and days divide.
My world is eight feet tall and eight feet wide.

I am lovely, I am lovely,
And my hair's the silken wing
Of a blackbird fluttering.
I am Lydia, Lydia Pritchett, I am lovely,
And my name is like a bonnet,
Velvet-crowned with feathers on it—
I am lovely in my bonnet,
And my hair's a blackbird's wing.
But who is it that keeps muttering?
Books? What books? There are no books here.
"Yes, sir, B shelf to the right."
(Your arms an engulfing hemisphere
To cradle my delight!)

And you, and you,
And you, and you,
Consult the file
For love's clear cue,
And dream hymeneal dreams the while.
Of unlearned lips and shaken hair
Learned in a consummating night.
"Yes, sir, B shelf to the right."
(Within your arms I swoon and quiver,
Then awaken with a shiver.)
There are no books, there are no dreams;
    these crushing walls are bare.

Turn back the clocks
Till once upon a time
Is here, and yesterday is now . . .

And now is a book-filled room where small sounds war
For listening ears, where windows dusk with night
And fluttering pages waken ghosts of flight.
Hear scraping chairs, and how footfalls explore
The muted range of echoes; through the hum
Of talk, the wheezing of the door
As searching readers come,
Their questions asked, and my routine replies,
The aggregate of twenty answering years.
Mark well the sameness, the unspoken whys,
The unfulfillment like a debt incurred,
The expected reparations in arrears,
The dreams that mock the payments long deferred,
The secret scourge of tears;
This now, this meager feast that does not sate,
The bitter blackened cup, the half-filled plate,
The sustenance of books upon the shelf,
Their passions gleaners' husks within myself.

And once upon a time is a cocoon
That dreams might spin around an afternoon
Turned of such silk as concupiscent weather,
The April urge of lovers come together,
Their shuddering clime, their equinoctial crest—
And now is the answering thunder long suppressed,
The consummate flood-tide's once upon a time
Begot of a dream, a dreamer's pantomime
Of courted limbs, of storied lovers taken,
Frustrate as never, fleshless as the shaken
And time-bleached bones of yesterday. Awaken,
Oh Lydia, to the emptiness of now.

Now is a square of silence and a lock,
Now is the rhythm of an unwound clock,
The deadly counterpoint, the year on year,
The sum of nothing, now, the dreamless here!

But what of that long ago grown echoless with time?
That music lost that measured out the days
In pulsebeat intervals; that nevermore
Of touch and mutual need and lovers' ways;
The body's richest season brought to prime,
Its ultimate pitch recalled, its culminant score
Of gone-forever cadences, that living rhyme
Of flesh on flesh, uncoupled now, its poetry no more!

And what of the dreams, the lost beyond the losing
As time or definition, east or south
Become as dust for one remembered mouth
Of summer ripeness textured for the bruising . . .
Now is the taste of dust.

And now is the sudden host within the walls,
Their black encampments challenging the light,
Their flighted arrows deadly parasols,
The torch of day extinguished by their night.
And now is the cowering body and no shield,
Forever now the quarry run afield.
Now is the dust and the unending dark.

Monotony's a room where living frets
The very flesh; wherein mortality
But merest breath sustains; where hope begets
But shadows, and defined totality
Is nothingness. Monotony's a room
To sum up silence, where the hours unwind
Like run-down clocks; where space and time assume
The walled, the never patterns of the mind,
The shape of dust. Monotony's a room.

What are the ways
To measure waiting?
What device may plumb
The soundless waters of expectancy,
Its tides of now and will-be correlating?
What calculator sum
The blind uncharted days
That merge to forfeit all identity?
Should there be none,
Is time, eclipsed and seasoned, once completed,
Forever clocked and tided, set to keep
Its subtle rhythms counted out and run?
Are hourly stragglers shepherded like sheep?
Are solar cycles ceaselessly repeated
To total all things ended once begun?
Shall waiting too be done?

Edge of Night

Translated, night's sheer
Hallucinate drifting
Is music I hear
And wind shifting;

Sidereal rhyme
That witches the senses,
Transcending time,
Confounding all tenses.

Awareness hovers
Along night's edge;
The body discovers
Dream's leverage,

Its destined euphoria
Deep and deep
In phantasmagoria
Hewn from quarries of sleep.

Beyond Loss

For Nat and Peter

Caught in dream,
They are always young,
Cavort about daylong
Dazzled by air
The color of honey.

Are yet serene,
Concerned only
With stickball score
Or ring-a-leavio,
Game ended or begun.

No hint of predator,
No sudden threat
Of disarray.
Locked in time
Beneath that lambent sun,
They are inviolate,
The dream never done.

IV

Where Small Birds Preen

Guinevere, The Nun

Repentance tastes of candle wax and mold.
Bereft of Arthur and of Lancelot,
She wears her griefs like garments, fold on fold;

Her proud head shorn, no longer aureoled
With diadem, and wreathed in bergamot.
Repentance tastes of candle wax and mold.

Not yet inured, she grapples in the cold
With lust and guilt, and rues what she was not.
She wears her griefs like garments, fold on fold

In this grey place where even time grows old,
And dreams that harry sleep are misbegot.
Repentance tastes of candle wax and mold.

As thoughts rebel, how winnow dross from gold,
Find grace in Ave or Magnificat?
She wears her griefs like garments, fold on fold,

And starves the flesh that will not be consoled.
Forsaken ease and panoply—for what?
Repentance tastes of candle wax and mold.
She wears her griefs like garments, fold on fold.

Mrs. Lincoln Speaks of Ann Rutledge

She claims him still
Who is no more
Than essence flowers shed
Within a room,
Or shadow spent upon a floor,
Yet opens doors at will
And comes between us,
Waking and abed.

I have no prayer
To exorcise a scent,
An echo, or the dream she spells
That lives behind his eyes;
Can proffer only
Fleshed embrace,
And tears upon
An aging face.

Afternoon at the Carnival
For N. who loved it all—In Memoriam

Awaken the calliope
And the spinning carousel,
The restive steeds
That rode the luminous air
On gilded hooves.
For you, my brother,
I would retrieve
The finite weather
Of that afternoon,
The sound and spectacle
Of midway revel,
Its flare and tinsel
And festoon.

Impelled by whim
Or distant trumpet call
Only you could hear,
You wore a wooden sword
To harry, slay
Whatever dragons were abroad,
And yet inviolate,
Vanquished sundry knights
We met along the way;
At last, just beyond,
Resplendent as Ophir,
The realm of carnival
Arrayed in light.

Reclaim them from oblivion—
Juggler who beguiled,
Clown who tumbled, dancing dwarf
No taller than a child.
Whirl the giddy carousel,

Horse with tasseled mane and bell,
Ring-a-round and ring-a-round,
All yet well.

Imbued with fantasy, we paused
At vendor's booth and tent,
Sleight of hand and barker's spiel,
Sideshow gambit lent
The artless guise of truth.
Mark how we braved the ferris wheel,
And ventured coin and faith
On games of chance,
Bauble, tawdry prize
Accounted rare
As emeralds from Zanzibar,
And pearls, and tiger's-eyes.

If prescience stirred,
We paid no heed,
Time and circumstance
Yet filigreed . . .
Remembered now
When light itself is dross . . .

I dream we ride the carousel
Again, again,
And you, my brother,
Long beyond sound
Of hoofbeat,
Sit astride and tall,
Your victor's brow crowned . . .
I reach out—
But dream and laurel wither
All too soon,
And bred of loss,
Nightmare shades abound.

Sabbath Portrait
For My Grandmother

Today is hers, the very light
Grown sacrosanct, her bearing free
Of fret-encumbered weekday plight;
Her Sabbath-bred serenity

Enriched by covenant and hymn.
Today is hers, its tenure fraught
With visions bright as seraphim—
Despair unlearned, belief rewrought.

Become inviolate with prayer,
Elect beyond the bane of woe,
She is transfigured, hers to share
Pledged Canaan, unwalled Jericho.

Love Song

Deprived of you,
I, who cannot bear
The flaunt of lilac
Now that I backpack
Grief, and wear
Leaden shoes,
Shall gather stones
Like lovers to my breast,
Stroke their cold foreheads
With desolate hands
That once cherished yours.

The Door

In some dark realm beyond the edge of sleep,
I dream an arcane door that is not mine,
And walk where stones afflict, and leaf shards heap
Their dooms around my feet. I crave a sign
That all is not yet lost, exhort the air
And castigate the stars, but they are dumb.
Deprived of will, must yield, each sense aware
Of that strange door, and night's delirium.
I crouch behind a rock, but searching winds
That bruit of snow intrude and seek me out.
I mount the stairs, and place my finite hands
Upon the latch—step into nothing—shout
Defiance as I plunge toward the abyss—
Then sudden grace, new light like genesis.

A Length of Rope

If you were brave
Or faltered, if you chose
To speak aloud or weep,
None bore witness save
The heedless rose
And windward sweep
Of unrepentant grass;
Bore witness
As time, finite
And forever, peaked
And ticked away
While you appraised
The height of tree limbs
With dead eyes,
And measured out
A length of rope.
Beyond prayer,
I chide the rose
That did not shriek
In protest, and the grass
Unmarred by disarray;
But my words
Are eaten by the wind,
And what birds abound
Wear noonday light
Like brass.

Keats Speaks of Fanny Brawne

Fanny Brawne, with whom Keats was hopelessly in love,
nursed him through several bouts of tuberculosis, the disease
that killed him at 26.

Fluttering her hands,
She patterns lies
That summer me
All out of season,
Enchant my apathy
Like butterflies
Veering toward light.

In this grey room,
Though nothing flowers,
My thoughts are shepherded
At her behest
Where sweet dews brim
Upon the hour,
And grasses dip and crest

Until recall intrudes
To strangle breath,
And all my senses cower.

Nineteenth Century Quilt
Los Angeles County Museum

What wisdom spelled your fingers as you shaped
This bit of cloth or that to fretted star
And flower? What litany of praise you kept

Behind your eyes? Attuned to metaphor
Your senses learned in verse or dream, you plied
Your needle, patterned love to cinnabar

And saffron flaunt of petal that defied
The silver wilt of frost. Your firmament,
Unmarred by cloud, yet dazzles, hope and pride

Stitched opulent as moons that are not spent,
And birds that wing and hover. Never known,
You touch my thoughts and greet, each briefly lent
Affinity of mind and heart and bone.

Change of Season—Lake Washington

The summer boats are gone,
And I like water
And the harried light
That spends too soon,
Wear a winter mien,
My thoughts imbued
With ultimates,
And suitably austere.

Awed by likelihood,
I reinvent my griefs,
Lament the absent bird
That does not skim the tide
Or grace the shore,
Am wrung by utmost leaf.

Not yet inured,
Berate the hapless air,
But sere afflicts the bone,
And winds impair.

Winter Come of Age

Decline and growth abide
Within the seed as one
To flourish side by side,
And feed upon the sun.

Each April ascertained
Is winter come of age;
In every bud contained
Its autumn heritage.

Inception's ultimate,
Yet origin withal.
Each phase is aggregate,
The end inaugural.

Where Small Birds Preen

Inimical
Though light grows tall,
And April urgencies
Tremble even
Beneath stones,
My human weather
Runs counter to such season,
And would refute
The quickening of grass.
Though I walk among trees
Where small birds preen,
I walk alone
Where you are not.
Though new light blooms,
And wings untether,
My thoughts so riven
And undone by loss,
Disavow flower,
And the silken stratagems
Of scent and hue and sheen.

The Gift

After the myriad
Rose-leaf summer,
After the spent moth
And plundered hive,
Mark how the turning year
Regales with asters
Tall as pride
Along the footpath,
And orange hawkweed,
And aureate grove.
How render tribute
For this late gift
Of panoply and hue
That tempers being?
Let me give praise
Before winter drift
Freights mind and bough
   and wing.

Now in October
For L. who is beyond calendars

Time garners loss. I linger at the gate.
Pruned neat, your dahlias glisten, court the sun,
The air yet gossamer, the season late.

My senses court pretense as shadows freight
The weathered light, and silken shrouds are spun.
Time garners loss. I linger at the gate.

What echoes roil the grass, what dooms, what spate
Of hapless footfalls spent too soon and gone,
The air yet gossamer, the season late?

Your roses pay no heed though I who plait
My griefs like garlands, listen, am undone.
Time garners loss. I linger at the gate,

Deprived anew by ultimates that wait
Even among your flowers. I touch each one,
The air yet gossamer, the season late,

And briefly rapt with wing. But dews abate,
And whispered leaves rehearse oblivion.
Time garners loss. I linger at the gate,
The air yet gossamer, the season late.

Sestina for a Granddaughter

She does not chatter now, takes chalk in hand,
And draws a house, invites me in for tea
We must, at her request, pretend to drink;
Contrives a door, delineates a lamp
To keep the dark at bay, a pot of flowers
She claims are roses, tries to write her name.

Caught up in fantasy, I speak her name,
Its syllables like music, take the hand
She offers me, pretend to smell her flowers
That never learned the rain, the scent of tea
And rose commingled as she flares the lamp
Whose light we share. We lift our cups and drink.

All hunger spent, her presence food and drink
Beyond the grace of bread, what need I name,
At once addressed. We revel, house and lamp
Rendered in chalk, transformed by sleight of hand
To likelihood, the benison of tea
Defined anew with doll-sized cups and flowers.

We court illusive season brave with flowers
No winter mars, whose perfect blossoms drink
Edenic air and draughts of dew like tea;
Invent a storied place we do not name,
And roam at will, affinity, her hand
In mine, and whimsy brighter than a lamp.

At length return, the·house and windowed lamp
As real to her as touch, her simple flowers
Accorded being, gentled by her hand
To summer redolence, and plied with drink
Lest sere intrude, and loss we dare not name . . .
Defer for now, content to stop for tea.

Her eyes entreat. I watch her fix the tea,
Counter the murk of shadow with her lamp
That lends an aura radiant as her name
To all within, to unsubstantial flowers
Purported to be roses. What we drink,
Charmed to ambrosia, what we dream—at hand.

Today is legend, apt with tea and flowers,
Our kinship like a lamp. My senses drink
And rally—hope, a cherished name, a hand.

SARAH SINGER's new book, *The Gathering,* embodies those outstanding qualities that have been the hallmark of her writing: exploration of a wide range of themes that go straight to the heart of contemporary experience, style and craftsmanship of a high order, and an underlying intensity of emotion and compassion.

Her career has been marked by an unusual succession of honors and awards in recognition of her achievement as a poet. For five consecutive years, the Poetry Society of America awarded her prizes for her poems. The National League of American Penwomen gave her first book, *After the Beginning,* the 1976 Marian Doyle Memorial Award for the best book of verse by an American penwoman. She has received numerous other awards for her work, and her poems have appeared in many leading periodicals and anthologies.

Among recent award-winning poems are: "The Exile," 1990 first prize for traditional verse from the National League of American Penwomen, Portland branch, and "Sestina for L.", 1989 Washington Poets Assn. award. In 1988 the Penwomen's Seattle branch presented Sarah Singer their Owl award for poetry.

She was vice president of the Poetry Society of America, 1974–78, consulting editor of *Poet Lore,* 1976–1981, and is currently secretary of the Seattle branch of the National League of American Penwomen.

A graduate of New York University and mother of two children, Sarah Singer now makes her home in Seattle, Washington, where she moved after the death of her husband, Dr. Leon Singer, a few years ago.